SPANKY IS ADOPTED

Written by Larry G. Johnston

Illustrated by Paula Tabor

U

Spanky's story begins on a warm spring day at a ranch in the village of Desert View, California where he was born. Bob, the ranch owner, came upon the small male donkey standing on unsteady legs next to his mother, Molly. Bob checked the baby over and determined it was a jack, or a boy donkey. Like all donkeys and mules, males are called jacks and females are called jennets.

This is Spanky, a miniature donkey

Bob patted Molly's back in a spanking motion and decided right then to name the new donkey Spanky. When little Spanky acted as if he was hungry, Bob walked back to the house. Molly and her new baby needed time together. Spanky's father was a spotted donkey who lived on a ranch in a nearby town.

Within hours Spanky's legs were strong enough for him to follow Molly out of the barn. Spanky investigated the big field adjoining the barn. There was no grass on the ranch because other donkeys had eaten it all.

Feed Barn

One morning Spanky ran around a small feed barn in the center of the field. Two more new gray baby donkeys ran after Spanky. All three babies were soon out of their mothers' sight but they came running back bucking and kicking up their heels. They made dust fly while having a good time. They continued running in circles around the barn until they got tired. Then the little donkeys laid on the ground and took naps in the warm sunshine.

The babies played and nursed for the next three months. Then it was time for them to be weaned. For weaning the baby donkeys were placed in a pen separate from their mothers. All three babies ran along the fence that kept them away from the mothers. The mothers, including Molly, ran along the fence on the other side. The mothers missed their babies and the little donkeys still wanted milk.

After a couple weeks of being in different pens, they all quit running along the fence line. The baby donkeys now ate hay and occasionally grass in the field. They received soft apple treats once they were weaned. They also received

Spanky with his halter

their baby shots and their teeth were checked to see if they were growing correctly.

The baby donkeys were haltered and petted to help them learn to be gentle around people. They were led around the ranch wearing their halters. Each hoof was raised off the ground and held there for seconds because donkeys must learn to stand on three legs to have their hooves trimmed.

Both of the two gray baby donkeys would leave the ranch soon. Spanky, the first baby donkey born, still needed a new home.

After Spanky was weaned, his mother was moved to a different ranch to be a companion donkey for miniature horses. A rancher wanted Molly to protect his miniature horses but he did not want, or need, a baby donkey. Donkeys can act like a guard dogs. They make a loud *braying* alarm cry when they see stray dogs or coyotes nearby.

In the next pen, Spanky had noticed two adult donkeys. One was a gray and white spotted jack named Al and the other was a light brown jennet named Darla. These two older donkeys would soon become Spanky's best friends.

One morning Ann and Harry arrived at Bob's ranch to look at donkeys. After looking around at most of the other donkeys, Ann and Harry decided to buy Al and Darla. Darla had already been trained to pull carts but Al needed more training to pull a cart safely.

Ann told Harry, "We need one donkey that is trained to drive so we can learn about driving too. We are new at this, just like an untrained donkey."

Harry agreed with Ann and said, "We will have to learn about driving along with the donkeys. We will have our trainer, Sandy, training all of us."

Ann and Harry continued walking to other pens looking at more donkeys. They came to a pen where they saw Spanky, who looked so lonely standing in the big pen all by himself. He was being kept separate from other adult donkeys so he would not be hurt. When Ann walked into the pen to pet Spanky, he nibbled on her shoestrings and fingers and nudged her forearm with his nose. Her shiny rings probably made Spanky curious.

Ann looked at Harry and said, "He is so cute, …. what can we do with a baby donkey?"

Ann and Harry both liked Spanky, so they asked Bob more questions and looked closer at little Spanky.

Bob said, "People look at Spanky but no one takes him home because he is so small."

The ranch had been sold so Bob needed to move. He needed to find Spanky a new home. Bob wanted Ann and Harry to take Spanky and give him a good home.

He said, "I will add Spanky to the deal with the two donkeys you purchased. He will be yours…you can just adopt him! You two don't have any small children."

Ann and Harry decided Spanky would go with them to their ranch. They hoped he would become good friends with Al and Darla.

Now Spanky was only half as tall as the two full-grown donkeys. By the time he was full-grown he might be around thirty-four inches tall.

Equines, including donkeys, get measured from their shoulders to the ground. Their heights are measured in "Hands." One hand is equal to four inches. Measuring is done from the ground to the top of the withers, or shoulder, using a measuring stick marked in hands and inches.

A miniature donkey, horse or a pony, measuring thirty-four inches tall is referred to as being eight hands, two inches tall. The thirty-four inches divided by four inches becomes eight hands with two inches left over.

Horses are taller and one could be five feet, four inches tall at its withers. How tall would that be in hands? A horse five feet, four inches is really sixty-four inches tall. The horse would be sixty-four inches divided by four, [one hand equals four inches] so that sixty-four inches becomes sixteen hands. That's taller than a miniature donkey.

Animals measuring <u>over</u> fourteen hands, two inches tall are horses. Those animals measuring <u>under</u> fourteen hands, two inches are donkeys, mules or ponies.

A measuring stick is used to take height measurements of animals.

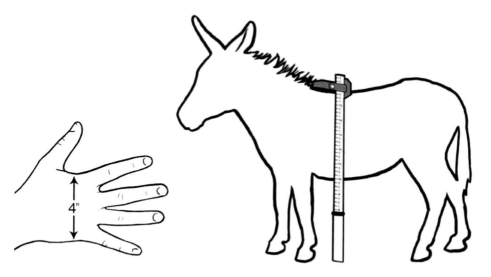

One Hand is four inches   Measurements taken at the Whithers

Two hands are moved, one above the other, from the ground, up the leg, and on up the body, to the top of the whithers, to take the measurements of equines. Each four inches of a hand's width is added to get the total measurement in inches.

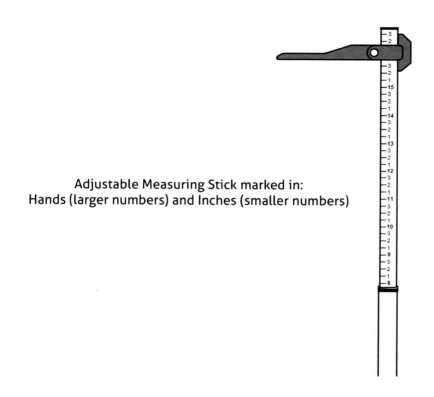

Adjustable Measuring Stick marked in:
Hands (larger numbers) and Inches (smaller numbers)

Today was a special day because Spanky, the little spotted donkey nobody wanted, was adopted. He went home with Ann and Harry to live at their new ranch with Al and Darla. Donkeys can live up to twenty-five years or more. Al was seven years old, Darla was now ten.

Bob hoped Spanky, Al, and Darla would enjoy living on a new ranch. Two days later he loaded little Spanky, Al, and Darla into the horse trailer. He would make the two-hour trip to deliver the donkeys to Ann and Harry at their Old Wagon Ranch.

The Old Wagon Ranch was in the desert town of Joshua Valley. At the new ranch the donkeys would have their own small barn, feed and water troughs, lots of toys, a salt block and nearly an acre of ground on which they could run and play. The large pen had a busy street along one side.

The donkeys saw lots of cars and trucks going by on the street. The trucks made strange new noises. These noises scared Al and Spanky at first because they had not seen many cars and big trucks. They needed to get accustomed to the new sounds, including the trash trucks and other big road equipment vehicles used to work on the street. Ambulances and fire trucks roared by with sirens sounding loud and their red lights flashing. Soon the donkeys learned to ignore these vehicle noises.

While competing at donkey shows Darla had seen lots of different vehicles so new noises did not bother her. Darla had travelled on the road riding in trailers and had heard many other loud noises.

At the new ranch, Spanky watched ravens and jack rabbits looking for seeds in the field. When he ran toward them, the ravens flew to the Joshua Trees. The jack rabbits ran away under the gate.

Raven

Jackrabbit

Coyote

When a coyote ran by in the field outside the fence all three donkeys watched and often brayed until it was out of their sight. Donkeys don't like coyotes.

Spanky and Al liked to play and explore everything. Their toys included orange traffic cones, blue barrels and small black tires. The two boys walked around, holding on to the same orange cone with their teeth. They also liked to carry their small black tires in their mouths.

Spanky and Al playing with a traffic cone

Darla showed little interest in the toys, but she watched the boys playing. As Spanky grew taller he ran everywhere and Al ran with him. On cool evenings, they would run and chase each other in the field and around the barn.

When they stopped running, they stood up on their hind legs to bite each other's neck or front legs. They both played rough and would bite hard. Al would bite the top of Spanky's neck and hold on while Spanky tried to get loose. Once he got loose, Spanky bit the top of Al's neck. He held on tight with his teeth just as Al had done with him. When Al broke loose, he ran away and Spanky chased him around the field and barn.

The little donkeys played and ran around kicking up dust. Darla usually just watched the two boys playing but sometimes she ran with them.

People driving by in their cars stopped to watch the three donkeys while they were running. The donkeys were a funny sight when they ran up a small hill and around the barn. From the barn, they ran along the fence and back out around the barn again.

They ran along the fence with Al in front running fast. He turned his head to one side to confirm that Darla and Spanky were still chasing him.

On dry days the dust kicked up by the donkeys flew everywhere. It was a sight, seeing the three donkeys running in the field at a full gallop. They ran around their small barn and out into the open field. On their return trip, they ran over a small hill and then around the barn again. They ran and ran until they got tired.

When they stopped running they rolled in the sand. They rolled from one side to the other side in the same sandy spot on the ground.

When they all finished running and playing Spanky took a nap. He would lay beside the barn in the sunshine. Because he was still young Spanky needed short naps often during the day. He needed to rest so he would be ready to run and play with Al and Darla again.

Spanky taking a nap

When sleeping at night the donkeys lay on the ground. They always slept near each other and they seemed to feel safe inside the large fenced pen. When the nights got colder they would sleep inside their small barn.

After eating their breakfast, the two older donkeys would stand in the sunshine and take naps. After taking short naps, the donkeys all explored the big field. They were looking for new things.

If donkeys were sleeping on the ground they might have to escape fast. They would need to get up on all four feet before they could run away.

The ability to sleep while standing upright makes it easier to avoid possible attacks by other animals.

Donkeys, horses, mules, and ponies can lock their knee joints and sleep while standing upright. They can also sleep laying on the ground. People cannot lock their legs to stand upright and sleep like donkeys.

Donkeys can see to the front and along the sides of their bodies. Their eyes are on the sides of their heads, unlike people's eyes which are in the front of their heads. This allows donkeys to eat grass on the ground with their heads low and still see possible danger approaching from either side, using each eye independently.

When Spanky got a few months older, and taller, he would go stand by the water tower and take his nap with Al and Darla.

Donkeys sleeping while standing

The two ranch dogs, Mickey and Lulu, barked at the donkeys when they ran around the big field making the dust fly in the air. Lulu was a black and white Shih Tzu and Poodle mix and weighed about twenty pounds. She ran faster than Mickey, who was a Maltese and Shih Tzu mix. She was the same size as Lulu, but a light brown color.

The little dogs didn't understand the donkeys were playing and having fun. Both dogs ran along their side of the fence barking when the donkeys went running past them.

Mickey   Lulu

Spanky had a lot of things to learn at the ranch. He would watch Al and Darla do cart training activities. Spanky was not afraid of most of the new things he encountered. He quickly became used to the ranch life routine and adapted well to his new surroundings.

Ann and Harry had become his special friends as they gave him apple and carrot treats and walked him around the ranch.

Within a year Spanky had become almost as tall as Al. He could now keep up while running with both Al and Darla.

One morning Ann commented to Sandy, "Right now Spanky is just a tall, long legged, lanky boy, …. he reminds me of a teenage kid. It is fun to see him growing and learning lots of new things; he has become my very special little boy."

Sandy agreed, "He will work out fine here. His driving training should go well as he learns quickly and he is easy to train. But he will not be strong enough to pull a cart with a driver seated in it until he is about three years old.

You two should just enjoy spending lots of time working with him because he is a very good donkey. Spanky seems to be happy at his new home with Al, Darla and everyone who stops by to visit. He really seems to like you and Harry."

One morning Ann saw Darla pawing the ground with a front hoof.

She told Harry, "Better check Darla's feet and see if she needs her hooves trimmed."

Harry checked Darla's feet and told Ann," Yes, you're right, it is time for hoof trimming. Her long neck mane hairs need trimmed too."

Ann called the horseshoer, or farrier, who normally came to the ranch to trim all of the donkey's hooves about every three months. When the farrier arrived, Ann and Harry put halters on the donkeys and brushed them. The donkey's hooves needed to be picked up off the ground and checked for small rocks.

A donkey must stand on three legs while one hoof is being trimmed. During the trimming by the farrier, small pieces of the outer hoof edges are cut away. This keeps the donkey's feet straight and flat along the bottoms. The farrier cuts off the hoof's outer edges with a hoof nipper and then uses a rasp to smooth the hoof's edge.

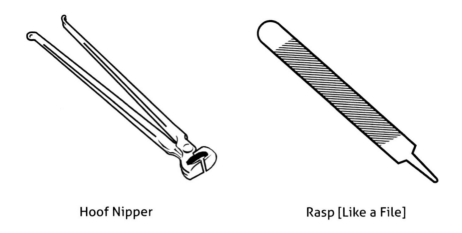

Hoof Nipper   Rasp [Like a File]

When the hoof and mane trimming began Al and Darla made snorting noises. They wiggled their back ends from side to side. They looked toward Spanky and brayed little, "Hee Haw's." Both were acting as if the trimming was hurting them.

Because Spanky had never had his hooves and mane hairs cut, he seemed to think he might get hurt and he became somewhat afraid of the farrier. Al and Darla had been playing a big joke on Spanky. They were only acting as if the trimming hurt. When it was Spanky's turn he soon learned the hoof trimming and hair cutting didn't hurt.

Rocks can stick in a hoof's bottom near a V shaped piece of the foot named the frog. Rocks stuck between the frog and the hoof's softer bottom might hurt the donkeys. A sore hoof can cause a donkey to become lame as they cannot walk with small rocks wedged in the bottom of their hoof.

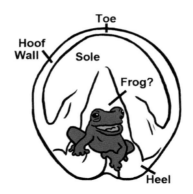

[No....there is <u>not a real</u> **FROG** in a donkey's hoof bottom]

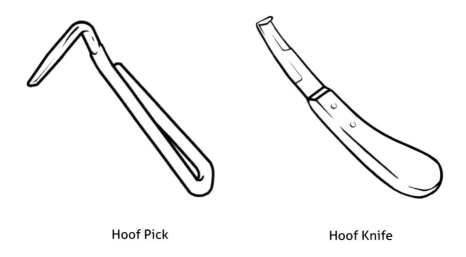

Hoof Pick   Hoof Knife

The farrier would clean dirt and small rocks from around the hoof's frog and then clean the hoof's bottom with the hoof pick.

Next, the farrier trimmed any excess growth from the bottom center of the hoof, near the frog. For this trimming he used a special tool called a hoof knife.

Equines hooves do not hurt when being trimmed. With the hoof work completed, the donkeys received an apple treat.

Miniature donkey's hooves are much smaller than big horses. Small steel horseshoes are not available to be nailed to little donkey's hooves.

When the farrier was done, Ann would use scissors to cut the donkey's neck mane hairs shorter, almost like a flat top haircut.

Cut off pieces of hoof removed by the farrier

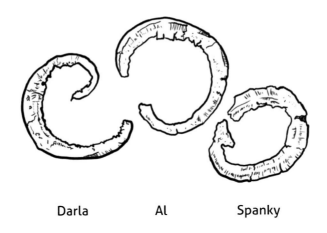

Darla   Al   Spanky

Al liked to lift his head high into the air and make a face. He would turn his top lip up so that he looked funny.

Al would then go, "Hee Haw, Hee Haw."

He was just begging for more apples after his hooves were trimmed. The donkeys chewed their apples and slobbered juice over their lips while some juice dropped on the ground. Carrots are not juicy, like apples, but the donkeys always seemed to like them too.

Al smiling and wanting more treats

Sandy trained the donkeys to respond to verbal commands. Training is necessary for two animals hitched together pulling a wagon to work as a team. Verbal orders are given to teach them to work as one because team donkeys need to respond together. Their training included verbal commands or directions for the donkeys to follow.

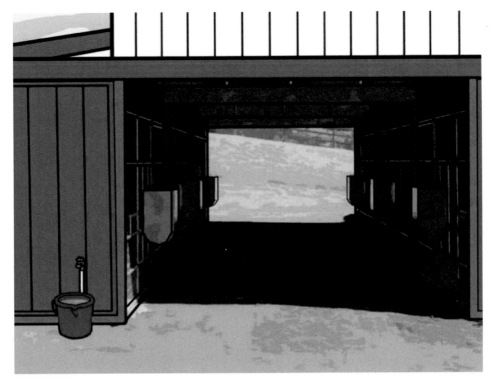
Barn's Dark Breezeway

While being walked around, Spanky did not like to go into dark shadowy areas. He placed his front feet in the dirt and stood with his behind up in the air. Spanky wanted nothing to do with the barn's dark breezeway. He refused to move, no matter how hard Ann pulled on his lead rope. Spanky acted stubborn as only donkeys can be.

Ann used carrots to persuade Spanky to follow her while walking him in small circles and finally into the barn.

She would softly say," Now come on Spanky, there is nothing for you to be afraid of."

With each small circle Ann made, Spanky was being moved closer into the barn's breezeway. Ann gently coaxed him to walk into the breezeway and as long as he was being distracted by carrots, Spanky wasn't afraid. He learned to follow behind Ann and walk all the way through the dark barn breezeway. Spanky learned to trust Ann and he would soon follow her anywhere.

Ann walked slowly while Spanky looked and sniffed at new things. Spanky now liked the big barn where he found lots of things to investigate, nibble on, and smell. He found small bits of hay on the floor, which he ate. He walked everywhere behind Ann while wearing just his halter and lead rope. Spanky was not afraid to walk on small loose gravel and smooth cement driveways.

Ann had to use treats to persuade him to walk through any small water puddles since he was still being cautious. Spanky became familiar with the ranch grounds because he was losing his fear of new things.

Ann and Harry took Spanky to see the veterinarian to be neutered, a surgical process to remove a male's testicals to make the animal unable to reproduce. At most ranches male equines are neutered to make them gentle to handle and train. Spanky stayed at Sandy's ranch and she exercised him by walking every day. Within two weeks he had healed and returned home to Ann and Harry's ranch.

On warm sunny days Spanky would stand in the barn with his head sticking out the doorway. Al and Darla would stand nearby, under the shade canopy.

The donkeys watched and waited for Harry to bring cut apples or carrot pieces. When they saw the small bucket in Harry's hand, they ran to greet him and get their treats.

Small Treat Bucket

Salt Block and Water Tank

All of the donkeys liked to lick on a salt block beside the water tub. The block contained minerals to help them stay healthy. After licking the block, they would all take long drinks from the water tank.

The donkeys received their feeding of hay early in the morning and again in the late afternoon. On some days they might receive a small amount of hay at lunch time. Their hay feed portion was weighed because too much hay would make them fat. The donkey's feeding time was scheduled near the same time every day.

Rick was the ranch hand who repaired things and kept the ranch grounds clean. Spanky seemed to think the manure mucking tub, with small rope handles, was just another toy. He followed Rick around the property biting on one of the two rope handles and pulling on the tub.

Rick would push Spanky aside with his leg while telling him," You're a nosey little pest, get away from this muck tub and let me do my work."

If he wasn't pushed away, Spanky would pull on one rope handle with his teeth and dump the tub of manure back out onto the ground.

Rick used the muck fork to pick the manure up again and then he dumped it into a small trailer. Later he spread the manure around to fertilize desert plants. Cleaning up manure was part of owning donkeys. It helped to keep pesky flies under control. Rick was lucky the small donkeys left small manure piles, unlike bigger piles horses left on the ground.

Spanky always followed Rick in the big field and watched everything he was doing. If small hand tools were left on the ground, Spanky would pick one up with his teeth and try to steal it.

Rick would say, "Spanky, you are a cute little guy, but sometimes you are just a real pain in the backside. You go play somewhere else and just leave my tools alone."

When Rick finished his work, he would always pet Spanky. He would lift Spanky's feet, scratch his long ears and talk to him. Rick really liked Spanky, even though he could be a little pest. Spanky liked the extra attention and Rick would give all three donkeys a small amount of hay from the feed barn.

Winter was over and Spring had arrived at the ranch. One sunny morning Ann hitched Darla to a new two-wheeled cart. Darla had not been hooked to a cart and driven for many months as it had been too cold during the winter season. She wore her bridle and harness instead of her halter. The harness had shiny brass color things that seemed to catch Spanky's eye. Ann walked around a few minutes with the empty cart following behind Darla to get her used to the cart's weight.

Ann then got into the cart driving Darla around the ranch property and into the big round ring. Darla listened to Ann's commands.

Spanky and Al watched Darla pull the cart. They both ran along the fence braying, "Hee Haw, Hee Haw." Al and Spanky seemed to want Darla back in the pen. She was out of their sight for a few minutes while behind the barn. When Darla was walking around in the big round ring the two boys could see her but they still brayed.

After training, Ann removed Darla's harness and brushed her. Ann told Darla, "You did very well for your first driving trip since last fall. Let's just see how you stand now when I check your hooves."

She lifted Darla's hooves to check for small rocks. Harry gave Darla her apple treats and returned her to the pen.

Al pulls a cart

I t was time to begin Spanky's driving training. He was two years old and he needed training to learn how to eventually pull a cart. Sandy started the training by ground driving Spanky. He would need to become comfortable wearing nothing but a halter with two driving lines. Later his training would progress to harness driving, tire pulling and finally cart pulling.

The training would be spread over a number of months as Spanky became stronger and used to performing his new tasks. Training is a gradual process over time where Sandy would introduce different tasks and commands during the sessions.

Spanky had a lot to learn. He seemed to like ground driving as he performed well with his new tasks. Sandy used a small whip to tap Spanky on his backside, when he stopped walking. He could only stop walking when Sandy told him "Whoa." He soon learned the whip was a reminder tool she used to get his attention, not to hurt him. He made many trips walking all around the big round ring while being trained by Sandy.

After weeks of ground driving, it was Spanky's day for a change. One morning, after being brushed, Sandy removed his halter to put on his new bridle. Then he had the steel bit placed in his mouth. This was a new experience for him.

Steel or aluminum snaffle style mouth bit

His new harness was placed on him. It needed minor adjustments to fit correctly. Spanky's two harness tug lines, used for pulling, were attached to a wooden single tree. Chained to the single tree's short center rope was an old black car tire.

Wood singletree with an old car tire attached

Spanky now pulled the old tire around in the big round ring. Dragging the tire scared him at first, but soon he got used to the noise and the tire's weight. The tire made dust fly and it bounced a bit while being pulled behind him. He learned to walk around in a figure eight pattern and in big circles while in the ring. The round ring was a safe place to keep him confined in case something startled him. He would be easier to handle while confined in the ring, should he get spooked and try to run away.

Spanky pulls an old tire

Spanky worked just fine in the round ring so his training continued with walking around in the big field. Spanky was doing his new job and pulling something, just as Al and Darla had been doing. Spanky seemed happy when he responded to commands of whoas, right turns, and left turns. He was having fun. He was also trained to just stand still, in one place, for a few minutes.

Sandy, an experienced trainer, had trained miniature donkeys for years on her ranch. She worked for short time periods with Spanky because he was young and he was easily distracted. She didn't want him to tire of his training lessons, so she was patient and gentle with him.

While driving she told Ann, "When Spanky lays his ears back it means he is listening to my voice commands. It doesn't mean he is mad, as some people might think when an animal lays their ears down and back toward their mane."

andy stressed that training had to be positive. She said, "Always end the daily training on a positive note... when Spanky had done something right."

After forty to fifty minutes, she stopped the training lesson for that day. Sandy spoke to Spanky constantly and said his name so he knew she was right behind him. Once Spanky was responding to commands and he was comfortable pulling a tire, he would graduate to pulling an empty cart.

Spanky worked pulling that old tire for many weeks. Then one day, to his surprise, he was finally hooked up to a cart. He was now doing the same thing as Al and Darla. The cart was empty, but Spanky did not seem to care.

Sandy walked behind the cart while driving Spanky, since he was not strong enough yet to pull her riding in the cart.

Training continued for weeks with all three donkeys being driven all over the ranch property. After training, the donkeys were brushed and had their hooves checked for rocks. Then all three donkeys received apple or carrot treats. When they were turned loose, they ran to drink fresh water from the water trough.

Months later, when Spanky grew stronger, Sandy would ride in the cart with him pulling her everywhere. Spanky practiced directions to "back up" and to "trot" while pulling a cart.

Spanky was quick to learn the new tasks and he was a pleasure to drive pulling a cart. Other people, watching him, said he was handsome wearing his shiny new bridle and harness.

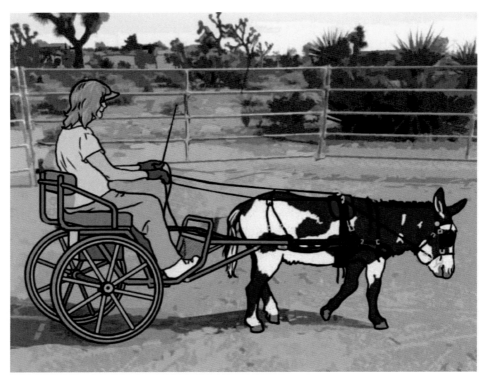

Spanky being trained to pull a cart

ꙅꙅꙅꙅꙅꙅꙅꙅꙅꙅ

Harry loaded Darla into the horse trailer on a bright sunny Spring morning. Then a new shiny buckboard was rolled into Harry's truck bed. Harry planned to drive Darla in a parade held in the town of Joshua Valley.

The town's annual Grubstake Days Parade was held to celebrate gold prospectors and the founding of the town years ago. Local people would ride horses and others would drive their horses pulling wagons.

Lots of other vehicles including fire trucks, police cars, classic cars and motorcycles were in the parade. There would be two or three bands playing music while marchers twirled and walked.

People dressed in western outfits marched in the parade along with lots of children who wore their special club's uniforms. People sat in chairs along both sides of the highway parade route clapping their hands and yelling at their friends in the parade.

In town Darla was hooked up to pull the shiny four-wheel buckboard Harry had built. The parade judges thought Darla looked very special.

Harry drives Darla in a parade

The judges had never seen a miniature donkey pull a small four-wheel buckboard. Darla was a big hit and everyone cheered and clapped as Harry drove her down main street.

Harry was excited and happy as he realized Darla was a good show donkey. She could pull the buckboard in big circles while in the street. She would go close by the spectators at the curbs, and then in big figure eight circles. Darla seemed to be enjoying the parade as much as Harry.

Western style Buckboard built by Harry

The judges all liked the small wooden buckboard. They had never seen one small enough for miniature horses or donkeys to pull. At the end of the parade, the judges gave Darla a *Blue Ribbon* for winning First Place for equestrian entries. Harry took Darla back to the ranch and gave her treats. Everyone was happy she had won a Blue Ribbon in the small-town parade.

Darla's Blue Ribbon

Harry, Ann and Sandy continued training the three donkeys with cart driving during the summer. When colder weather arrived, both carts were returned to the big barn until the next spring.

Winter brought occasional snow to the high desert. The donkeys would stay near their small barn until the snow melted. All three donkeys had grown heavy winter coats of hair so they would stay warm. The donkeys all walked around the field after it had snowed. They put their mouths into the snow to lick on the top. Often, they would bite and roll in the snow.

On early cold winter mornings, the donkeys would stand in the field near one corner of the ranch house. When a house light was turned on the donkeys brayed, "Hee Haw,... Hee Haw," wanting their breakfast. Harry had not yet had a sip from his first morning cup of coffee.

He would look out the window at the braying donkeys and tell them, " You noisy little donkeys just be quiet, I will be out to feed you soon. You don't need to wake up all the neighbours."

After Harry got dressed in his warm clothes, he headed to the barn. All three donkeys quickly trotted from the house toward the barn to get their morning hay. Harry never got to oversleep as he always heard the funny little, "Hee Haw's."

He often wondered, "Can those smart little donkeys really tell time?"

Spanky seemed to like the noise made while he bounced and dragged a small barrel in the field. He could pull the barrel with his teeth by holding on to a rope Harry had tied to the barrel's top. Dragging the barrel left a visible mark in the sand and one could see Spanky had been playing with the barrel.

Ann and Harry often sat on the patio after sundown laughing when they heard Spanky dragging and bouncing his barrel around in the field. Spanky was the only donkey to drag a barrel as it had become his special toy.

Spanky drags a barrel

On rainy days, the donkeys stayed inside their small barn waiting for the rain to stop. They didn't want to get wet nor did they like being outside on windy days. The small barn kept them dry and out of rainy or windy weather.

One morning Harry placed the horse trailer in front of his workshop. He left the loading platform down on the ground. Then he put a small bit of hay on the trailer's front floor. Al and Darla went into the trailer to eat hay but Spanky seemed unsure of what he should do. He would not go inside the trailer even to eat hay. Al and Darla had been inside a horse trailer many times. Spanky had only been in a trailer when he was delivered to the new ranch.

Ann told Harry, "Put some hay on the loading ramp."

When Harry put hay on the loading ramp Spanky ate it. Next, he placed a small pile of hay on the top of the loading ramp.

Spanky took two short steps on the ramp to reach the hay. He had to stretch his neck out as far as he could. Once he reached the hay, he ate it all.

Hay on the trailer ramp and floor

Spanky now seemed to feel safe when Al and Darla were inside the trailer eating hay. Harry led Al and Darla out of the trailer and held them both off to one side.

Harry told Ann, "Put a small pile of hay on the trailer's front floor. Then Spanky will have to go all the way into the trailer to eat."

Ann dropped more hay on top of the loading ramp and the trailer's front floor area. Spanky walked up the ramp to get to the hay. He ate the hay at the top of the ramp and then walked into the trailer and ate the hay from the front floor.

Ann then removed Spanky from the trailer. She had him practice walking up and down the trailer ramp to get in and out of the trailer. After some practice walking on the ramp to get hay, Spanky was no longer afraid. He had learned to load himself into the trailer to go on trips.

All animals had to learn to enter a trailer in case of an emergency, like a brush fire. They would have to be taken away from the area in a trailer to a safe place.

ⵣⵣⵣⵣⵣⵣⵣⵣⵣⵣⵣⵣⵣ

One day a friend asked Ann, "Why don't you bring Spanky to visit the seniors' home where he can walk into their rooms?"

Ann and Harry soon began taking Spanky to the home and the residents gave him small pieces of carrots or apples. Everyone at the home liked Spanky, the little spotted donkey. The people always asked Ann and Harry to bring Spanky back soon.

Spanky became a big hit at the seniors' home. The residents often saw cats and dogs but seeing a spotted miniature donkey was unusual. They all seemed to enjoy Spanky's visits to the home.

One weekend a school teacher was driving past the Old Wagon Ranch when she saw the donkeys in the field.

She stopped, rang the doorbell, and asked Ann, "Do you ever take your donkeys on school visits?"

Ann replied, "No, we haven't thought about it. Harry and I just enjoy driving all three of them here on the ranch."

The teacher invited Ann to bring a donkey to school for the children to see. Ann talked it over with Harry and they decided to call the teacher soon and make the trip to the school with Spanky.

Later when they took Spanky to school all the children liked him. They asked questions and got to pet Spanky and feed him carrot pieces. Spanky seemed to like all the attention he got from the children.

Now Spanky had another job, he went to school to make friends with young children. Spanky made trips to various classes each school year.

All the children and teachers enjoyed Spanky's school visits. Ann and Harry held a short class in the parking lot to teach the children about donkey care.

After a couple years of making school visits the school staff awarded Spanky a *Goodwill Ambassador Certificate.*

Ann and Harry were very proud of Spanky and all the friends he made at the school and the seniors' home. He had become a real asset to the small desert community.

Ann and Harry answered questions from the children about what donkeys can do, what they eat, and how long they live. The children learned donkeys can pull carts and some can give rides to small children.

On some school trips Ann, Harry, and Sandy took Spanky, Darla, and Al to school. All three donkeys got to visit with the children, school staff, and teachers.

Ann and Harry were very pleased they had adopted Spanky when he was small. He had grown into such a good, even-tempered donkey. Spanky seemed to enjoy his two friends, Al and Darla. He also liked his visits with older people and school children.

Often Ann and Harry thought they might try to compete in donkey driving shows. Spanky, like Darla, could become a good show donkey pulling a two-wheeled cart.

After more specialized training, they thought he could also pull a longer style, four-wheel buckboard. Spanky could then be driven in some of the local parades and maybe win his own blue ribbons.

Winter was coming to the high desert again. Spanky had grown his long coat of hair to keep him warm when the temperature dropped to freezing at night.

Ann told Harry, "Spanky looks overweight now. I guess it is just that long hairy coat he grew to keep warm. Come spring he will look like a slim donkey again when the winter coat all falls off. He will be a different donkey then."

Now Spanky had nothing to do but keep warm and healthy. Next spring he would shed his long coat and begin running and playing with Al and Darla again. He would make trips to see the senior citizens, school children and meet the people who stop by the ranch to visit. He would continue his training to pull a cart and maybe a buckboard wagon.

For right now, he would just be content to eat his special treats and of course, any grass he found growing on the ground.

THE END

BIT - mouth piece for control of animals

BRAYING - the "hee-haw" noise a donkey makes

BRIDLE - a leather strap item on horse's head for control

BUCKBOARD - four-wheel wagon with a flat bed

CART - two-wheel horse drawn vehicle

COYOTE - a dog-like animal

EQUESTRIAN - a rider of any equine

EQUINE - a donkey, horse, mule, or pony

FARRIER - a horse foot specialist (see **HORSESHOER**)

FOAL - a baby donkey, horse, mule, or pony

FROG - a piece of any equine's foot bottom

HALTER - a head harness to control an animal

HARNESS - leather components to hook animals to wagons or carts

HAY - dry grass to feed animals

HOOF - donkey, horse, mule, or pony's foot

HOOK UP - to hitch an animal to a wagon or cart

HOOVES - donkey, horse, or mule's feet

HORSESHOER - a person who puts steel shoes on horses (see **FARRIER**)

JACK - a male donkey

JACK RABBIT - a long-eared rabbit

JENNET - a female donkey

JOSHUA TREE - a tree that grows in the desert

LEAD ROPE – a short rope hooked to bridle or halter to lead animals

LINES - leather straps to drive animals <u>pulling</u> wagons or carts

MANURE - animal droppings

MUCK CART - a small cart to hold a muck tub

MUCK FORK – a wide end plastic fork used to pick up manure

MUCK TUB - a plastic tub to hold collected manure

NEUTER - removing male reproductive parts

REINS - lines to drive animals being <u>ridden</u>

SALT BLOCK - a block of salt including minerals for all animals

SHADE CANOPY - a cover to protect animals from the sun

SINGLETREE - a wood piece on a wagon to hook, tug, or trace lines to

SNAFFLE BIT - a metal bit with a jointed center and a ring on each end

TRACES - lines from a harness to a wagon or a carts singletree (see **TUGS**)

TUGS - lines from a harness to a wagon or carts singletree (see **TRACES**)

WAGON - a four-wheel horse drawn vehicle

WHIP - long leather item to tap on an animal's backside

ABOUT THE AUTHOR

Larry G. Johnston fell in love with miniature donkeys while attending miniature donkey and horse shows throughout the west. He liked their cute, friendly, and affectionate nature. He met Spanky after building The Old Wagon Ranch in southern California when Spanky became one of the residents.

Larry's early years were spent in St. Louis, Missouri. Later, his family moved to a small farming community where Larry attended high school and worked on a horse ranch. After serving as a Navy submarine torpedoman, he went on to graduate from the Los Angeles Police Academy. He worked as a police officer in Missouri and in California.

After earning his bachelor's degree in Psychology and Law from Southeast Missouri State University, he worked at a juvenile institution and as a high school teacher in California. After more than thirty years of public service, he retired as a Lieutenant from the Orange County California Marshal's Department. He now enjoys traveling throughout the United States in his R.V.

"Spanky Is Adopted" is the first in a series that will follow Spanky's antics and adventures.

If you enjoyed the story, be sure to leave a review or email the author at l.johnston377@aol.com

Thank you for reading!

ABOUT THE ILLUSTRATOR

"We couldn't afford a horse when I was a kid, so drawing was the next best thing"

...is how Paula Tabor describes why she started drawing horses. "When you've sat on a fence drawing horses and one tries to take a bite out of your sketch pad, you're hooked." (True story - got the boxy teeth marks on the cardboard to prove it!) And this is why she continues drawing them.

Paula Tabor lives near a ranch in Houston, TX where 400 rescue donkeys live. Illustrating "Spanky Is Adopted" was a natural fit.

Paula Tabor is an award-winning portraitist, illustrator, and caricature artist. Her contributions to the "If You Were Me and Lived In…" series; "...Elizabethan England," "...American West" and "...Mayan Empire" won a 2018 National Indie Excellence Final and a 2018 Feathered Quill Book Award.

www.PaulaTabor.com

Made in the USA
Las Vegas, NV
23 January 2024